LUCAS
FISHBONE

———————●———————

LUCAS
FISHBONE

BY GREGORY MAGUIRE

ILLUSTRATIONS
BY FRANK GARGIULO

HARPER & ROW, PUBLISHERS

The author wishes to thank the
staff and family of Blue Mountain Center, a writer's colony
in upstate New York, in whose nurturing midst
Lucas Fishbone first showed up.

Lucas Fishbone
Text copyright © 1990 by Gregory Maguire
Illustrations copyright © 1990 by Frank Gargiulo
Printed in
the United States of America. For information address
Harper & Row Junior Books, 10 East 53rd Street,
New York, N.Y. 10022.
Typography by Andrew Rhodes
1   2   3   4   5   6   7   8   9   10
First Edition

Library of Congress Cataloging-in-Publication Data
Maguire, Gregory.
   Lucas Fishbone / by Gregory Maguire ; illustrations by Frank Gargiulo.
      p.   cm.
   Summary: The imaginary Lucas Fishbone fosters a special
relationship between a grandmother and her granddaughter.
   ISBN 0-06-024089-X : $. — ISBN 0-06-024090-3 (lib. bdg.) :
$
   [1. Grandmothers—Fiction.]   I. Gargiulo, Frank, ill.   II. Title.
PZ7.M2762Lu 1990   89-39772
[E]—dc20   CIP
                                                          AC

Over the river and through the woods—
This is the year I know the way,
All by myself, to Grandma's house.
First time—all by myself.

She's waiting at the orchard gate.
Gingerbread lions and birthday balloons
And cranberry juice in a plastic jug,
Arranged on some paper towels on the grass.

Grandma says, "Can this be you? You've grown so tall!"
I think she's angry—maybe she doesn't *like* me tall? But
she hugs me around from front to back, and kisses me extra
for my new inches. I'm back at Grandma's, back at last!
Then we plop ourselves down for the birthday snack.
"Why are there three places set?" I say.
"Oh, Lucas will come," says Grandma.
"Lucas who?" I say.
"Lucas Fishbone, that's who."
"Lucas Fishbone *who?*"

"Lucas Fishbone, gentle beast,
Come by water, come by air.
When he gets here, what a feast!
Oatmeal bread and beans. At least
Thirty kinds of chocolate bar.
Lemonade and lettuce. Pear
And pretzel. Jam and jelly, jar
On jar. And Lucas standing there.

"Did you call him King of Beast?
Lucas? Hah! Not in the least.
Lucas Fishbone doesn't rule.
Hums and strums instead. Or rhymes
Thoughts you never hear in school,
Words that promise glory times!"

After a while Grandma takes the leftovers up to the
house. I can see Lucas as if she's drawn his picture in the
grass. I think she is in love with him!

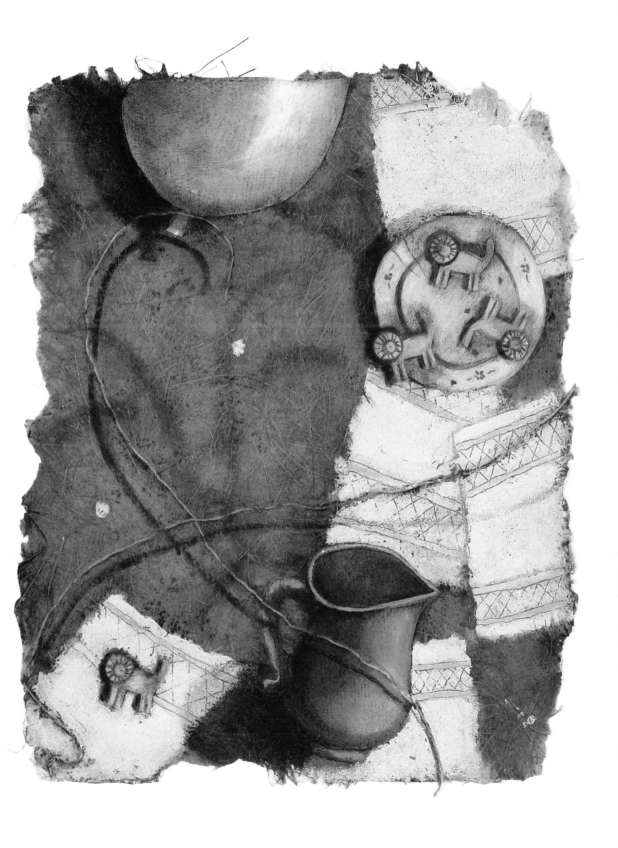

When I'm brushing my teeth and she doesn't
know I'm listening, she sings:

"Bobby Shaftoe's gone to sea,
Silver buckles on his knee.
He'll come back and marry me—
Pretty Bobby Shaftoe."

But this year I think she's dreaming of Lucas Fishbone.

Spring, on school vacation, when the road is too muddy
for cars, I walk up the hill till I can see Grandma's roof.
My boots are off by then, and I give my feet
their first mud bath of the year.

Grandma, planting, sings to her little ones:

"Lucas likes a little shoot—
Curl below a curving root,
Grow a pleasant crimson beet.
Or straighten up and send a sweet
Leaf of green and lend a fruit.
What you give to eat, we'll eat,
And set aside a bit, to boot.
Lucas might be right along.
Every spring I hear his song."

She puts her ear to the watering can as if it's a
telephone, and laughs when I laugh at her.

"I think we should put a fence," I say. "Or the animals will eat it all before he gets here."
"We save some for the animals, and some for us," says Grandma, "and some for Lucas Fishbone. And some we'll can and send to town for the old people who like fresh beets and beans and greeny things."

"You always talk in rhyme," I say one night. Grandma rocks. "Lucas taught me." She sews a new head for the scarecrow. I stuff the body with straw and give it my boots for feet, because the mud is drying out and I don't need boots now.

"He looks too mean," I say.

"He'll keep the crows off," says Grandma.

"They can have their seed where I throw it for them,
but not from the garden." "If Lucas comes, it might scare *him*."

"Lucas doesn't scare so easily."

But she gives the scarecrow a bright bandana,
and the garden is ready to grow.

Summer: I run. Everywhere, water!

"Sprinkler in the morning.
Swimming hole at noon.
Sudden shower for an hour,
Supper's coming soon.
Thunder during salad,
Lightning during cheese.
Lucas Fishbone, for dessert:
Rainbow sherbet, please!"

"Where'd you meet Lucas?" I ask Grandma.
"In the market where I grew up," she says.
"I was buying *klompen*—wooden shoes for working
in the garden. He made me up a song to sing while I worked."
"Sing it to me," I say.
"Never you mind," she says.
"Some things are private."

But after a rainbow Grandma feels more chatty. She
brings gingersnaps, and we dig up rocks for a rock garden.

"I was young, of course," she says, "and not so fat."
"You're not fat!" I say because I love her.
(But she is, a little.)
"He said to me, 'I'll take you for a spin.' And he rode
me home on a bicycle. But I had to take care of my mama,
who was sick, so I didn't go riding with him again."

"Let's build a rock seat for you and Lucas Fishbone,"
I say.
"Maybe it'll be *you* and Lucas Fishbone," she teases,
but we both know better.
It's a little bit lopsided, but if we squeeze we
can both fit.

At night Grandma kisses the picture of her mother
before we go to bed. I kiss Grandma.

It rains at night, too. Like pebbles on the roof.

Fall.

They call it Fall, and leaves fall, of course. But they
could call it Rise if they wanted.

Geese rise, and honk good-byes.
Time flies.
Wind lifts, and calls, and lifts, and sighs,
and lifts leaf curtains in the skies.

I see Grandma on Halloween.

We carve a Lucas Fishbone face on the pumpkin.
A candle glows in its friendly eyes.
Then Grandma sets the dough to rise.
Bakes bread. Makes pumpkin soup, and pies.

"I'm starting to rhyme all the time," I tell Grandma as
we paint each other's faces. She is being me,
and I am being her.
"I know," she says. "If you're being me, you can answer
the door tonight. Maybe Lucas Fishbone will come."
Lucas Fishbone in disguise!

Little creatures all through the dusk. Just as if the
guests of Grandma's garden have grown a little bigger and
found shopping bags in the woods.
A chickadee. A pirate fox. A hen with
drooping woolen socks.
A scarecrow!

Grandma is tired. Now I know how to light the stove,
so I heat up some apple cider with cinnamon sticks in it,
and we stay up late, watching a movie on TV.

"I need to clean out my closets," she says, full of energy the next day. "Fall is the time to give clothes to the poor. This old dress, it's warm as toast. Someone will like it."

"But isn't that the dress you wore when you went dancing with Lucas Fishbone?" I say. "You showed me once—"

"Lucas Fishbone will recognize me no matter what I wear," she snaps. "Pack it up."

I'd like to save it for myself. To steal it, even. But Grandma has an eagle eye, so I fold it neatly in the box.

Winter wears white.
Fur around the eyebrows of Grandma's house. The eyes
of a warm fire in the hearth, every night, and in candles.

We decorate the tree outside the porch. I've brought
three dozen silver balls from town. Grandma makes her
popcorn strings and a holly wreath. She rocks and sings:

"Oh, the rising of the sun,
The running of the deer,
The playing of the merrie organ,
Sweet singing in the choir."

She doesn't make up her own songs so often now,
but the old ones are good enough. Good to hear,
in Grandma's crackly voice.

One day she wraps her wooden shoes up in newspaper
and ties a big red bow on them, and leaves them
on the piano stool where I find them.
"But Grandma! I can't take these!"
"Take them, take them. They're guaranteed a lifetime.
They're made from trees," she tells me.
"You might want them when Lucas Fishbone comes."
"You do your practicing," she tells me, "and
I'll sit on the couch and listen for mistakes."

We make oranges stuck around with cloves.
One each for us, and twenty-two to send to the nurses
going overseas this month, so when they're far away
and troubled, they can smell winter at home.

Lucas Fishbone, Lucas dear,
Come by water, come by air.
I would greatly love to hear
Just one song—a word—a sign!
Come by water, come by air.
Any way you like is fine.

Another spring, a new pair of boots two sizes larger,
but mud the same as mud always is: muddy.
I carry my wooden shoes in my knapsack.
No sense ruining them.

This spring it's like all seasons at once.
Spring mud, summer rain, fall breeze, winter fire.
(Grandma is always cold now, and no wonder,
with all the rain.)
We keep putting off the planting, and play
Go Fish instead.

To tease Grandma, I say,

"Lucas Fishbone's gone to sea,
Silver buckles on his knee.
He'll come back and marry me—
Pretty Lucas Fishbone."

"Pretty who?" says Grandma, worried.

"Pretty Lucas who?" "Never mind," I say.

She points out the window. "Pretty deep water out there."

"Our garden is a flood."

She won't be stopped, so she pulls on my last year's

rubber boots, and I pull on my own new ones,

and out we splash.

She tries to sweep out the water so she can plant pumpkin

seeds for next Thanksgiving's pies. It's no good, though.

She sits on our stone bench with the scarecrow drooping in

her arms. I start to take down the tree decorations, all

tarnished from being out since the holidays.

Lucas Fishbone!

Come by water!

Grandma stands up straight and waits.
He looks like the best old friend she ever had.
Just as dapper as she used to say.
And I can see a small stove just inside,
so she will be warm.
I never made the feast she promised him. All I have is
the packet of pumpkin seeds! No oatmeal bread or beans,
or beets or gingersnaps.

Lucas Fishbone, Lucas dear,
I am also waiting here.
Send me word of one I cherish
Who in leaving does not perish.
Come again another day,
Come by water, come by air.
Any way you like's okay
If you have Grandma with you there.

While I wait, I put down roots.
I will make some beet pickle to send
to Grandma's old friends in town this year.
I'll make some Lucas Fishbone gingerbread cookies.
And I'll make some rhymes.